𝒲 A R *is not the* S E A S O N *for* ℱ I G S

Lidija Cvetkovic was born in the former Yugoslavia in 1967 and came to Australia in 1980. After working as a teacher, she completed an Arts Degree at the University of Queensland and currently works as a psychologist in Brisbane. She has travelled widely in Europe and the Middle East. *War Is Not the Season for Figs* is the winner of the inaugural Arts Queensland Thomas Shapcott Poetry Prize (2003).

*W*AR *is not the* SEASON *for* *F*IGS

LIDIJA CVETKOVIC

UQP

First published 2004 by University of Queensland Press
Box 6042, St Lucia, Queensland 4067 Australia

www.uq.uq.edu.au

Typeset by University of Queensland Press
Printed in Australia by McPherson's Printing Group

Distributed in the USA and Canada by
International Specialized Books Services, Inc.,
5824 N.E. Hassalo Street, Portland, Oregon 97213-3640

 Sponsored by the Queensland Office
Queensland of Arts and Cultural Development
Government
Arts Queensland

Cataloguing in Publication Data
National Library of Australia

Cvetkovic, Lidija.
    War is not the season for figs.

    1. Australian poetry — 20th century.
    I. Title. (Series: Arts Queensland Thomas Shapcott
    poetry prize; 2003).

A821.3

ISBN 0 7022 3484 2

For my Nana

CONTENTS

3. LUMINOUS

ACKNOWLEDGMENTS

Some of the poems in this book (some in earlier versions and with different titles) first appeared in the chapbook *War Is Not the Season for Figs* (Vagabond P, 2001), in *New Music: Contemporary Australian Poetry moongalba — poems in honour of oodgeroo*; and in the following journals: *The Age; Overland; Heat; papertiger; Poetrix; Social Alternatives; Divan; Australian Multicultural Review; Five Bells; Linq;* and *Jacket.*

I am grateful to Dr John Leonard for his commitment and faith in my work. I would also like to thank Dr John Knight, Judith Beveridge, Dr Martin Duwell, and my peers in Brisbane for their advice; my boss Peter Kohleis; and my husband Mark Medosh for his understanding and encouragement.

This book was completed with the assistance of Arts Queensland grants and a Varuna Writers' Centre Fellowship.

I

RELIABLE MAGIC

WAR IS NOT THE SEASON FOR FIGS

We spent summers at the Adriatic coast.
We learned to tread water and float; the shores
were covered with stones that jostled for room
the sea's surface mirror-still.

Thanks to Tito, *our violet blue, daisy white,*
we were content enough with sour cabbage
and garlic on our tongues;
and figs — huge and fragile as babies' heads.

Once, fig in hand for a friend, across the stones
I twisted my ankle and fell.
The fig split open like a heart in my palm.

Now I want to retrace my steps:
drive from Budva to Dubrovnik to Zadar;
but I hear they've shifted the stones
built walls that segregate by blood
and god and name.

On street corners gipsies proffer
their cupped hands as they always did,
while arm in arm with priests and saints
Tito makes a spiritual comeback.

The figs have shrunk in size
they lie beneath neon lights — cold, shrivelled, green.
War is not the season for figs.
Only fools offer their hearts on a palm.

A PORTRAIT OF MY FATHER

My father draws a blade
along the wired frame
as we watch perfect rectangles
of honeycomb topple into
a stainless steel bowl.

From a hard earned
78 centimetre TV screen
a voice fires … *massacres mass graves*
like bullets into our lounge room
shooting father. Blood
thick as honey runs along
his fragile frame.

On the antenna outside
crows congregate for attack
on the raw liver and heart
he set out as bait.
Father waits by the shed,
air rifle aimed, and fires
a bullet of revenge.

Long ago in his motherland
as he dozed beneath a poplar,
a snake supped nectar
from his angel trumpet ear,
the translucent vessel
of his wisdom. He foresaw
the scenes that flash
before us on the screen.

So we packed our grief and
headed for the land of his dreams
the step-motherland
who'd gag his deepest cries
with lumps of creamed honey.
I watched my father's tongue
sink to the clay riverbed
of his mouth like a stone.

My ageing father
nursing his swollen knees
collapsed under two decades
of laying tiles, when at dusk
he'd return throwing dollars
in the air like pollen.

My father
rescuing drowning bees
and ducklings from his pool;
stuck in the prickly middle
between mother and me —
calling truce between
the warring sides;
bringing in honey
unaware of the sticky
trail he leaves behind.

COLLATERAL, BALKANSKA ST.

She exists at the periphery of vision
where birds slice a crescent of sky
in their homeward turning,
where lovers part at the crossroads.

She is of water and air, of bread and salt
her eyes in low grass like moths
their wings folded against sunlight,
etched with frost. Still as in prayer,

foetal on the pavement, her knees
dormant iris bulbs, dark as chestnuts.
Her arched spine props God up.
In the earth her forehead takes root.

Her ear nests the resonance of footsteps.
She lives for the length of a glance —
she's an afterthought,
an echo.

If I were to shelter her beneath the eaves of my brow,
curl her in the nook of me
and offer the gift of my palms to her body,
my palms two lovers parted —

the drum of her pulse may lead them back
to the crossroads of her breast bone
to rise and fall with her chest, to rise and fall
and never forget the pledge that is her heart.

OBSERVATIONS ON THREE VARIETIES OF SNOWFALL

1

The first kind is not good
for making a snowman.
Dry and willed
its flakes the size of spit balls
it swoops like a mother in spring.

But if it happens to nest in astrakhan folds
it leaves the sheep to bring up its children.

It bites and will squeal if stood on.
If hordes walk over it
it takes revenge.
Dangerously compact
it can crack heads.

It has a long life
despite its meanness.

2

This kind is soft —
the size of chestnut-breasted cuckoo's eggs.
It falls voluminously.
It falls like plumes or ash.
It can be found on the tongues of children
or on the threshold of an eyelash.

No-nonsense scholarly types
standing wide-mouthed before the sky
are observed during snowfall of this kind.

It can be gullible.
In with the wrong crowd it snowballs to a fist.

In the limelight of a street lamp
it crowns every girl a princess
then helplessly falls at her feet.
Its brothers turn themselves into confetti
and inaudibly applaud.

3

The third kind can fall up.
Like a nectar-filled lorikeet
it traverses the earth
with vagrant wind and sun.
Nothing much becomes of it
it doesn't leave a mark.

It falls in warm weather
from expectant skies
and is especially nice upon waking
in someone's arms.

The largest number of unaccounted sick days
are recorded in this kind of weather.

The elderly and the sick stand by windows
as if there were fireworks or homecoming heroes.

It is festive and welcomed
because it's the earliest to arrive

because people forget the first kind.

RELIABLE MAGIC

When you go looking for the Cape York Lily
steer clear of the lagoon sister, for there
amid the reeds' hush, baby spirits murmur
of a coup — plot to plunge and lodge inside
your womb when you crouch to scoop some water.

I offer you an amulet, a necklace of yak bone;
push this sea sponge as far as it will go
and you won't need to squat and sneeze
or leap with heels to buttocks. Take no heed
of the wiseweak men who scorn my methods —

trust my magic as you trust the moon's return.
Melt the sulphum sap, ancestor to the fennel,
in the warm spring beneath your tongue; feast
on ground acacia leaves, honey mixed with dates.
But if you find yourself bereft of faith, lift the lid

to auntie's box, for hope still waits herewith,
Widow Welch's pills, a glass syringe holding
pearl ash, alum, sulphate of zinc; sea-weed pencils,
a gold wishbone, or silver ring; and the bouncing
Dutch Cap — once inside reliable, catch it if you can.

RIVALS

I'm having an affair
with poetry.
My husband is jealous
of the intimate hours we spend together
behind his back.
When the two of them meet
one tears the other to pieces.
With maturity
there'll be less hostility;
but for now I must give up my hopes
for a *ménage a trois*
and keep them far apart.
When we all slept in the same bed,
the two of them on either side,
I'd fondle my lover
when he woke me from my dreams
but the after-poetic glow on my face
gave it away. My husband tells me
I'm being used, cannot understand
why I give so much
when I get so little in return
tells me I should write a novel —
take it long and slow —
but I've always had a thing for quickies
it's the intensity that gets me.

REACH FOR THE MOON

A woman curves in the moon's circle
arms round folded knees
head bent, long hair in her lap;
her body projected
high on a white screen
folds over and over itself,
swivels and swells
in twelve stills
completing a full revolution —
from behind
her bare back is the full moon
from the front
her dark hair the eclipse
and from the side where
her breast meets her thigh
the white sickle of her back
cradles darkness.
Just when you think
her body will unfold
to show her face, it closes up
and a new cycle starts.
You can stand there for a very long time
waiting to see her face
believing it has something to reveal.

OODGEROO

Your elders saw beyond themselves
when they planted lemon seeds
in the ground at Moongalba,
while you left books of poems
for the future generations.

In a mass of silken thread that holds life
you wrapped your gift of words as
a golden orb spider wraps her eggs
beneath a curl of bark.

You were born of the barely audible
unfurling, splitting of silk.
You wove your poems, a sturdy web
to capture the wood-moth's struggle
the shriek of bird and bat.

The wheel stands high and taut
it supports the waning moon
holds the memory of *Mirrabooka*
in droplets of morning dew.

On Moongalba lorikeets and bluies
flicker in paperbarks, dip their beaks
into flowers, their heads tilting forward
at the angle of someone reading
feeding off the nectar of your poetry.

BRISBANE LEAVES

many no longer resemble themselves

this one curls on its side
it nursed a grief

all tattered edges, one abandoned itself
caterpillars grew fat off it

blown in from elsewhere
this one seeks the bough's asylum

one's veins splayed on the pavement
masses glance and walk past it

victim of a storm, this one wilts
away from its mob

multitudes are attacked
by gangs of aphids and thrips

this one dies on the crown
in the prime of its life

this one many a colour
death becomes it

II

THE PROCESS OF SEPARATION

THE FUGITIVE

When a man is grateful
to a river for his life
she carves her bed in his skin —
her undertows will always
pull him off his course.

It was a dandelion that did him in
when its cluster-head of seed blew up.
He still flinches watching horses
step across a paddock.

His soles map the escape.
Fear sharp as a tamarisk thorn
lodged in the tender arch of a foot;
even now he checks his tracks
for blood on the bitumen.

Inconceivable:
here he can walk for days
in a single direction
without crossing one checkpoint
border control. He walks

and finds himself yet again
at some river's edge, not knowing
what has happened in between
only that the moon has risen
water lapping at his knees.

ONLY SKYWARD

Were it not for the shadow our house cast
across the yard with midday —
were it not for the body's drive towards warmth and light —
were it not for the sun the earth my blood the sky —
i may not have shifted from that spot

                                              where

a bomb

                                      dropped

seconds

        after   *my rising.*

Give me back my house without its shadow,
my arms and their embrace
let me in just to see if any seed's pushed through the rubble,
how tall the tree;
to retrace the path from my first step
which taught me grass and wood and stone,
to my last which stole the ground beneath me.
Maybe then i would feel home again on anyone's land
not look only skyward.

THE YEAR OF RETURN

A caravan of exiles shifts across
the home town like cloud shadow.
They're back to reclaim their land
cautious as birds before an offering of crumbs.

Their sun cold-shoulders them
the street corner turns its back, windows
evade their gaze as cords release
blinds drop guillotine-quick —

time has crocheted a lace membrane
sparsely thread;
the sight of smallest things
catches on skin —

a doll on the garbage, her plaits intact;
tatters of the dress she wore for him
flowering on the rubble; map of cracks
on the ceiling they always meant to fix.

Through the window a stranger's shadow
in retreat; a smudge of his breath
on the inside of the glass.
It starts to rain on the other side.

ESCAPE

1

I awake to havoc in the yard.
Overnight winds have torn the gourds off a vine.
As I gather their pulp and seed
I hear the morning news —
they may be sending ground troops to Kosovo.
That's it: no more certified excuses. He'll be drafted.

> *Do you remember the bridge we cycled across*
> *that summer — the bridge across to Jasika?*
> *You were fifteen —*
> *It's been bombed. Live targets were guarding.*
> *I knew two that died —*
> *Are you still there —*
> We were cut off.

Since I cannot redeem the beauty of the yard
I head for the park. Gums peeling themselves back;
their smooth limbs the pallor of death.
Blood licked and matted, fine as a newborn's hair
strings of bark.

At the edge where lantana spreads
the tunnel has burst its rusty throat — a torrent
where drips had echoed from the hollowed dark.
At my approach a heron, dipping its charcoal beak
into the stream, retreats.

2

At first it was a tingling then pain in his arm
till he couldn't hold a gun or pull the trigger.
The paralysis made him useless. At home
he recovered feeling in his arm
when he began to sew and write.
Now he takes sedatives at night
stands by the window watching 'fireworks'
across the Belgrade sky.

In the monastery he lights candles
for the living and the dead, prays to the God
he's come to believe in … *let's meet in Amsterdam
on a bridge* — *Let's* — though he knew as well as I
… but it's dreams keeping him alive.

OPERATION STORM

each morning i must stand up to it
straighten these sheets
for some occasion
these are strangers
but what's to be done
with war now war

stand up find a reason
see my suit — it waits
these are not my hands
soft palms idling away
my earliest days stained
stained my last

i shut tight the taps
thought we'd be back
thought we'd be back
only asked for water
with so much water
and the wreck of his tenderness

shut the windows before we left
grabbed two bags
he was thirsty on the way
his skin puffed up
with so much silence
sunk beneath an air raid of rage

sometimes i lose my way
pick wild strawberries to sell
up in the forest i found him
shards of sky in the humus
didn't want to emigrate to Iceland
was all he'd said

feel as though I'm floating
late in spring my hands are red
one of ours, eyes still open
he didn't like the cold
didn't like the cold
all he'd said

SACRAMENT

i come back to where i left myself
to find an absence in my place

call out my name, but the echo
mispronounces it

i question a leaf — the wind expels it
peel back the skin of paperbarks

cicada shells cling to my sleeves —
beggars in the churchyard

i shelter one in the vestibule
of my right palm, beneath the steeple

i make of two fingers and thumb
to cross myself

light a candle and look back
my shadow has no head

i lift a rock to a panic of ants
beg them for a crumb of sacrament

SEVERED

Conversations with my great-grandmother

1

What was it like when you were young?
War had left its talismans …
From forests and fields we brought in
bombs and metal wrecks —
a strange sort of harvest —
to melt and shape and sharpen
into picks, sickles, axes, ploughs.
We trusted neither land nor sky
and prayed and crossed ourselves
whenever in the open.
We grew cherries, sold cheese
wove hemp into rope and cloth;
we thanked the lord for the corn bread loaf
coarse as it was it glowed like a jewel
in our mud and straw hut.

What was it like to be a woman back then?
My lot could not afford a daughter,
though I washed and scrubbed and loved
them all I could. On my wedding day
when I clung and cried, my mother consoled,
'You'll wear a cotton skirt there
you'll eat bread made of wheat, white as snow'.
As I rode off on the cart drawn by our cow
the accordion began to play, I turned to wave …
but the sky had collapsed behind you.

And on our wedding night …
First night and he found the frayed seam of you.
He pulled loose a thread to undo all you'd stitched up,
when in a tangled mess I fell at his feet,
'Don't waste your tears. The land is dry.
We're out of salt. Cry me a barrel by morning!'
I faced the next day split as a fallen fruit, plum-blue.
You became an ice-crusted country
Your voice a fish that nudged in the deep.

Year after year it was so … with him devastating
and you picking up. He felled saplings, spoiled crops,
with a deluge of fists he pounded down.
In secret I collected seeds, sowed and tilled the land
I knew so well in darkness.
I carried the sting of nettle, the strength of oak.
When it got too much, my eyes would follow a fly
spiral up. As it'd settle in a corner
something in me would still with it.

Was there a God?
It was useless with God. When first I turned to him
he spat it was my lot! Even the saints betrayed me.
Sweet martyr Paraskeva, giver of sight, whose icon
I adorned with flax and birch, turned a blind eye.
So I called on the Great Mother, 'Strike
with your lightning! Turn him to stone! Cut
the thread, his life you weave', I called into a hole
that with bare hands I'd dug.
Silence but for the echo of your plea
the crude snigger of crickets.
I sought a gipsy for a curse — 'Scoop the dust
from his footprints wherewith he leaves his soul
cut a lock of hair, his powers it holds, and coat
with clay or mud. As the flames crumble mud to dust
so will wither he.'

31

The axe was your last resort?
That night I breathed relief — an empty space beside me.
He kept the spare axe under the mattress —
I felt its head at the small of my back
the handle braced my spine.
Skipping the ritual of plaiting and looping
covering my hair with scarf, bareheaded
I tip-toed past my little ones to look for him in the yard.

It was another drunken night with mates and booze and cards.
He'd passed out beneath the cherry tree
where I found him sleeping soundly
and blossoms falling, falling …
I crossed myself for forgiveness
more out of habit than faith,
I gripped the axe handle
lifting it above my head —

2

Twelve at the time, standing at the window above
her daughter counted
while she fingered a wart on her thumb,
'How like a toadstool', she mused
as she set about to uproot it, ' … five six seven',
by the time she drew blood she'd counted the last thud.
Twelve resounded in her head like a spell of sleep
till the buzzing of a fly brought her back
and she heard the familiar drip from the white belly
of cheese hung in a gauze sack,
'Now like a cherry bitten in half'.

GRANDPARENTS

They say my grandfather as a young man
had enough strength to plough the entire sky.
When I was a kid, this giant, under my command,
sowed seven of the brightest stars. Yet

in a backdrop to this pastoral I can see
my grandmother drawn along the ground
her shoulder blades the blades of his plough.
My grandmother made the best bread —

she kneaded moon-flesh, waited for it to rise
in the warmth of her kitchen. When she delivered
nothing less than the full moon to the table, he would
bless and break it. In the idle winter months

she threaded sunlight through the eye of a needle
embroidered designs on white hems of fields,
on frills of eaves, tracing the somnambulant stirring
beneath the cover of her skin. In the summer

she split the bitter husk and dug him out a son, scooped up
little walnut dripping birth syrup, but the umbilicus
strangler fig, gripped with a twist the slender stalk
his head a blue bud never to fully flower.

And my grandfather did what no man of his time
would have done, when with needle and thread
he stitched up the threadbare rag of sky, and sewed
a patchwork constellation to cover his child and wife.

THE PROCESS OF SEPARATION

She drains the honey
the knife blade scrapes
along the wire that holds
the honeycomb. She cuts

chunks of it, cups the hollows
in her hands, the colour of old
whiskey. Taut our silence,
taut as the bare wire.

I grew too large for it —
my old summer dress,
roses dotted on storm indigo;
she's made a sack from it.

We grab handfuls of honeycomb
clench our fists around it
to collapse the used cells
to fit more into the sack.

The last of the honey
trickles through the fine gaps
the sickles of space that remain
between the fingers.

My fingertips are stained indigo
from pressing into the cloth.
Glad she found a use for it.
I think of it as a honey-stomach.

It's a process of separation,
she explains as she dips it
into boiling water, the roses
grow darker, the wax surfaces.

She sways the honey-stomach,
and through the steam
I strain to see her face
as she rocks the sack of waste.

BABA YAGA PAIN CYCLE

Back

Your breast against my back
lying on our sides, I camouflaged
the private ceremony of my body's grieving
while you skated into sleep …
all your mirrors bare and clean.

Back to back we formed an arctic landscape.
At my nape you chiselled a hole
to fish in the discrete waters of me.
Amid oil spills and whale blood
I clenched, shooed the fish nudging at the surface.
I gave you just a soggy shoe.

The small of your back always sore.
Each day I'd tip out water
in its place light a flame
with the rim of the glass to your skin
I'd seal the heat in to draw out pain.
This is how we recognise each other —
circles branded on our backs.

Ear

It was the ancient remedies we looked to
when pain became unbearable.
You poured warm milk into my earlobe
or furled newspaper into a cone
prodding with the pointy end
at the tender entrance of pain's dwelling.
As you set the open edge aflame
the strange comfort crackled and curled
rushing towards my head.

I did not flinch nor fear burning
for you'd flattened my hair
to my skull with water.
You released the hum and buzz
from the hive of my cochlea
seduced the snake from its grip on my heart
with your white lukewarm love
you flooded the tunnel with venom and honey
when you grazed against its swollen walls.
I know you didn't mean it.

Eye

Those times I'd wake up
with my eyes sealed shut
and feel for you, call you through the dark …
foetus-blind I'd fingerprint my way
along hallway walls, root-strewn forest floors
to your hut. But you'd cast your shadow
across the moon, you forbade me moonlight.

I heard your hut spinning in the wind
before it brought you news of me.
I felt my way along the fence,
children's bones for pickets,
I heard you scrubbing the stumps —
the four chicken legs supporting your hut;
I asked you for some water,
just a little water to dissolve the sap
that had sealed my eyes,
but you lied your well was dry
your body the only vessel
that held any water. Lick open my eyes,
I pleaded with you, lick open my eyes!

And you warned me that I would see
only as you see, as you held my head
in both your hands, your rough tongue
over the sealed line of my lids
over the smallest of my veins.
And I saw myself diminishing
as you fled in your cauldron towards the sky
sweeping the tracks in your wake;
I saw myself, wide eyed and small
in the pupil of your eye.

THE WHITE

He lacquered a hard wood table today
slowly, towards his body and away
the length of each brush stroke
stretching to the perimeter of pain,
and knowing him, that bit beyond.
In his voice I heard the once familiar
tenderness, like his face at the airport
after a protracted absence. And there
I was again, sky high on his shoulders
with him looking up at me, the white
of my knee-highs blending in with
the white of his shirt, as if I was
growing out of him, as if there were
no edge lines to my beginning and his end.

What held us both up
now barely holds him alone.
Uncertain of his body's ability
he leans on me to take his first steps,
and then remembers mine, when he
arched low over me like a willow,
like my very own rainbow. At sixty
he was still climbing palms to put up
Christmas lights, helping his wife into bed.
My tender, careful father
his backbone soft as a paperbark trunk
his vertebra crushed, looking up at me
from hospital linen, and I want to
raise him out of that white —
I want to raise him in my arms
and piece him back together,
make him resinous, make him shine;
but I just sit by him on the edge, and let the white
take me in, dissolve the space between us.

POST-DIAGNOSIS

Self-righteous as a squatter and just as streetwise
it moved into the cupola of my left shoulder
the whitewashed architecture a perfect medium
for the plexus of its dark calligraphy, for its graffiti.

I was weaving the naive brocade of puberty
still unblemished by iconography, when it perched
on the pillar of my humerus, carved its niche, patron saint,
parasite. The insidious chipping has thinned me.

LIFE SUPPORT

1

I've left all my belongings, all that resembles me behind:
the cat's needy meow, your calloused grip …
I've left the blocked pipe, the Poinciana in the yard
whose roots threaten like the unspoken between us.

The flowers here are scentless, and I hygienic
as the wash basin, as this motel linen, free of my clothes,
hairstyle, my name — stripped to my sheet-white bones.
In sleep, roots weave round my ribcage, push into my throat

when I go to speak an owl's hoot, a flutter of wings.
The coiled ear of a spring listens from the mattress' insides
heartbeat amplifies. I awake to left-over dreams,
the familiar taste of your earlobe.

2

In a laundromat amid the din of spinning
someone is peeling a mandarin's inner skin.
An old drunk with a gripe against the government
mumbles something about polio and war. A shirt whirls

now and then the sleeves fold round, mimic an embrace.
In the distance through the glass a man hooked like an ibis
roams beneath the strangler figs. He is looking for something
he has lost. His walking stick supports him.

3

I collect armfuls of stones, seaweed's interlaced geometries,
bones of birds long dead. Exiled by the ocean
bluebottles dry on the shore line, sprawl like suicides
or porno stars, trail their blue veins.

At the airport you wait for me. Your freshly shaved face
shocks me. I've brought you the elegance of stones,
I go to say, but you touch my hand, and I ask instead
about the pipe, has the cat been fed.

LOW TIDE

we stand at the end of a jetty
gulls scavenge our silence

i point to a pelican in the distance
you hold the horizon numbly

i offer you a remnant of sea life on my palm
the wind snatches your glance

you worry i'm retracing past loves
i scoop footprints off the sand

i call you to me on the soft ground
you run into the ocean's arms

you poke a jellyfish for signs of life
it recedes with the tide

an avocet points to something in the sky
all her sisters look up with their beaks

a woman sits by the estuary
asking questions of her cuticles

THE PEEWEE

A flash of black and white wings
was all I saw of it as it struggled
against the jet of my scream.
I remember a single mangrove
rising from the water;
a woman on the shoreline,
the tilt of her cheekbones
supporting the horizon; I noted
the solidness of them; wondered if
you'd see the miracle in this —
when its beak pierced the soft white
my immediate crashed brittle — it betrayed —
had I been blinded so close to my iris
the cushion of it, the peewee's bill a pin in it
hand over my eye calling for you, and tears
with their own will — a racing track
a carnival on my face.

It took this to soften you towards me.
In the calm aftermath, settling on your face,
a Vaseline haze as in romantic films,
still my hands kept making
the same involuntary gesture of defence
towards your touch as towards the sky,
and I saw the shoreline assert its edge
against the surge of water; I saw
a woman walk away, the horizon
waver in her absence as if about to collapse.

III

LUMINOUS

LUMINOUS

1

An Arab introduces himself as Sam
to a Dutch nurse on holidays from Baghdad.
While she chain-smokes the night,
he watches her bare calves flex.
The moon spills its amber syrup
cracks its porcelain shell
and she crosses and recrosses her legs,
won't speak to him till he tells her
his real name.
The smoke chokes even the stars.

2

The war is too close.
CNN purrs in the background
like an alley-cat scavenging scraps.
Intermittently bomb blasts illuminate his face.
She searches it for signs of love
but the light never lasts long enough.

3

Dawn's quiet
Then the fist of her heart
punching through the doors of sleep.
In the dream — his hand
a match
his hair his face
in flames
his features losing distinction —
flashes of it
through the morning call to prayer.
And she tried to put him out
but he remained luminous.

A SEED, A CRUTCH, A HEART

1

from the pig's slit throat a red carpet unrolls
all his life he's been fed for this

the matron of honour lays birds' eggs in her braid
they'll seal the nuptial kiss with their hatching

the bride's kin descend from the hills making wide gestures
with splintered hands, carrying the scent of humus and wolves

they meet at crossroads and laugh through the ruins of their teeth
as they hand the groom a gun

when he shoots the apple off the bride's head
a seed flies into her eye and grows into a seedling

clumsy virgins flirt with guests' lapels, pin rosemary
for fidelity, flaunt drops of blood from pricked fingers

the bride holds back from pulling a loose thread
off the priest's vestment lest it unstitch him

she back-flips her bouquet towards a young widow
marked with mourning, but the wind blows it back

the groom's hand mounts the bride's over the knife
his thumb crushes a frosted rose beneath the arbour

when midnight snips the marionette strings
the bride and groom collapse, cannot hold each other up

the groom chops the slender apple tree
and carves crutches, etches a heart on her iris

2

an apple tree grew from youth's eye
youth saw through its white bow

an apple thumped youth on the head
youth was never the same again

they cut the apple tree to protect youth
somebody etched a heart on the stump

that's all that remains in youth's eye
and a flicker now and then

ROSE OF JERICHO

Love me outside
                    where seed pod crescents sway
where poinciana tassels weave a delicate brocade
where boughs fall and break. I want the damask
of your lips, the attar plumes of your breath
to raise me, to rush me open, to make me whole
at the pitch of fracture.

                    A curse clipped short my wish
                    the voice fragile and violent
                    coming from next door;
                    I threw my head back —
                    a shudder of bottlebrush spray
                    the yellow mask of a miner.

Then you held me, we let the breeze slip
underneath our blanket like a pet, and I dreamed
of the fragrant garden we would have —
of oleander and figs from the hills of Petra,
acanthus leaves from the columns of Jerash,
of atra, cardamom, thyme, and mint …
And the Hills Hoist next door whirled like a dervish
its polyester florals and stripes irreverent
in their tangle, their slips of intimacy.

There is a gate in the fence that connects
the two territories, our neighbouring yards;
a quaint relic — its missing hinge, rusted latch.
Last spring I carried shears over this threshold
to my rose bed. I've often thought of taking back
a bloom in gratitude, but now it's too late —
I let the common rose tend itself
the bed overgrew with weed.

On our honeymoon in the Middle East
we bought a desert flower —
rising to a cupola, a shrivelled fist of root-like petals —
'Hand of Mary' the hawkers called it touting its powers.
True enough, we witnessed its resurrection:
in a glass bowl by our bed, submerged in water
it unfolded the mystery of its eternal return
the weight of it —

what if nothing were transitory,
what if there were no single moment,
what if a curse recurred
at that pitch of fragility and violence?

THE BODY'S INNUENDO

1

At first I only sensed the obvious —
in the body's crypts there were signs
but I couldn't read their textured meaning —
there was nothing but the shedding season.

I mapped the crests and troughs
looking to heat to tell me the seasons;
but the knowledge was always retrospective
(you only know the highest point
once you have fallen — and because)

I'd carry the sky in my pocket-mirror
if my iris would flush lilac in the bower.
I'd grow a sparse black lace of plumes
from my elbow to my wrist, speckles on my skin.
Instead I must decipher this body's innuendo.

2

We row in the shallows, suggestion of shadow;
tannins' wash of gold makes luminous beneath
ornament of rotten log, grace of stone.
We glide beneath the bellies of water birds.
Effortlessly they double themselves
in the water's black stillness.
The repetition of ripples, comforting
as when your tongue through the dark of me
like a leaf fallen in sweet water.
Loops of light sew the skin of paperbarks.
Without rain the logs will elbow through
to the harsh light of day to become dead-wood.

3

You hold my hand through the slit of plastic curtain.
The doctor comments on my socks and my
womb appears on a screen, displaced there,
lunar, strewn with shadows.

I wish for a better reception as she
takes the measurement, the egg's diameter.
I turn my head to the side — through the window
a frangipanni blooms; I can almost smell

its sickly clusters of scent. The sky
presses down with all its grey weight.
I feel your fingers come to life
as I clench my fist around them.

HOMECOMING

You can never go back,
only onwards into the world
leaving behind all the loved things
— DOROTHY HEWETT

The place we leave behind is Chagall-like:
the burst and lustre of the circus tent,
the invisible trapeze: mother, a firefly
embroidering the sky with silken
threads of her body's flight

and father rides through the hoop of fire
a winged Zephyr throwing handfuls,
gusts of laughter like petals
into the glass bowls of our mouths.

If Chagall painted the place we leave behind
Brueghel depicted it upon return: Icarus
in his mess of wax and feathers, a speck in the ocean
behind the ploughed brown.

The circus packed up now, but for the fat lady
her ankles swollen as clouds, she watches a feather
held by the wind, float still, resist
the pull of blue beneath.

SNOW DANCE

Remember this photo of us
slow-dancing on New Year's eve —
your arms slope down
to rest on my shoulders my head
is level with your breasts
the edge of my skirt
whirls at my ankles and is
fringed with the same silver and
red of your dress (breathless yet?)
though the black and white
doesn't show the thread
we share doesn't show
my hair striving
from my
shoulders to be like yours
at the lower back.
You
are looking down towards me
as if you'd said something
teasingly or tenderly
but my head is turned away
to face the camera.
Are they snowflakes at the window
ferries in the distance
witches shooting stars

or just dust on the lens —
let's say it was snow piling up
high to my waist in the
old year reaching up to yours
by the new to meet your black
hair at that bare-back dress
snow closing us in
closing us in and my arms
enfold your waist rest
in the nest at the small of your
back as you sway in dance
your hair laps against me no
gap between us except for
my gaze — turned away
the shock of flash
open shutter twelfth strike
too late —
snow and midnight
seize our embrace.

RETURN TO BELGRADE

In this grey town, Popa's
'white bone among the clouds'
the buildings stand still
like shocked witnesses.
Pigeons coo in the ruins of a high rise.
Amid dandelions and debris
a security guard dozes in the sun
in his hand a cigarette smokes itself ...
pigeons overhead, ash in his lap.

Refugees sell Lucky Strike
and Marlboro smuggled in from Kosovo
they can smell a cop a mile off
can disappear in a blink.
They are the invisible people
they are the dirty laundry
in Milosevic's basket piled underground
far from the hole in the wall
where he drops his bundle.

Meanwhile, in full light of public eye
Slobo's making links
crossing bridges he's rebuilt
bragging of progress
to visitors from the East.

Everybody's working on an exit scheme.

In an internet café a guy with dreads
extrapolates the physics of tofu
to a blonde bombshell
who's sipping Nescafé — the latest thing
to hit Belgrade since the air raid.

On a street corner a woman, barefoot
sings old socialist songs —
Druze Tito mi ti se kunemo
da sa tvoga puta ne skrenemo …

Nostalgia tugs at the heart of a man passing by

the heart which lies behind 'I Love USA'
rebellious on his t-shirt,
and he drops a Deutschmark
at the altar of her feet. She kisses him
not for the Deutschmark but for paying his respects.
A red smudge brands his forehead
like once a star.

SOUR CABBAGE, ROSES & LIES

After a decade of absence it's the crumbling
facades that strike me — chunks of paint split off
like states on the map of former Yugoslavia.
In the tenement flats everyone is spring cleaning —
tapestries, quilts, rugs expel the odours of winter months.

Uncle Uros, not uncle by blood but by virtue of his age,
welcomes me the traditional way: a teaspoon of preserved
quince with a sip of plain water, a shot of plum brandy,
and a cup of Turkish coffee. Dark sediment shifts invisibly
as we talk. To close the ritual we turn over our cups.
Fate unfolds before us.

He orients me on the city map
marking crosses where bombs fell, following with pen
the 'charred alley-ways' of his beloved Belgrade.
He'll be off at dawn to queue for sugar —
The worst thing's the company in these queues
the fools who swear by Milosevic to the grave

while he pockets their pension.
I too had a chance to emigrate, but the state offered us
this flat ... then my wife died. It was then he planted
the mass of roses by the wall. Over the years
he's guided them to cover the cracks.
April now. The wall exposed; mere buds.

Next day uncle Uros's knee is bleeding —
something about a slope and rain and a neighbour who
was supposed to help and the son who hadn't called —
Liars the lot of them! I ask about the opposition rally
while dabbing yellow on his flowering knee —
A mere two thousand, if you believe the Politika.

And the familiar smell I cannot place — *Sour cabbage*
(of course!) *from the basement where we crammed in*
round pickling vats playing cards and chess when the blasted
sirens kept us up. One good thing, young Slobodan
learned to play chess; I let him have my king now and then.
I'll be damned if I let his namesake win in September.

He is finished! Traitor to his own name. We'll pickle him!
When his knee stops bleeding, he pours us sljivovica —
To clean the blood from the inside. In unison we sink them —
To life! And he totters off to tend the roses, while I
feel the blood rush, my cheeks bloom.

INTERNAL EXILE

Winter's iced them in — pensioners in tenements,
an odd chestnut on the pavement;
beneath Danube's ceiling of ice fish gasp,
tap on the border. Their tapping is inaudible.

Bombs slumber in the river's bed of silt;
a resonance rhythmical as footsteps
in a bridge's broken ribs. Children throw stones
in the shallows, crack the shell.
Cigarette butts bob up for air.

Amid sculptures of metal jutting out from the ice
the war-fattened skol scotch, burn matches
down to the end — flames lick their fingertips
ice cubes melt under their breath.

Then there's winter's gentleness, her stasis,
her smoothing over with the white of forgetting.
She tucks in coke bottles strewn on the banks
as if they were orphaned babies.

What will be exposed, come thaw?
Will the Danube break again — spill its capillaries
to redraw the blood-map, the wine stain
across Serbia's face? Will the birds return?

*   *   *

On the riverbank two old men count crusts of bread
from a mesh sack, fight off crows.
Broken glass glitters around them
catching the first spring light.
They are breathing — you can see it from a distance.

NOTES

A Portrait of my Father. In Slavic mythology a snake licking the ear is a symbol of prophetic knowledge.

Baba Yaga Pain Cycle. Baba Yaga is an Eastern European pagan deity — the mother goddess of death and renewal. Ancient Slavs believed the eye to be the seat of passion and emotion, and the ear the location of reason or even life itself.

The Year of Return. 1998 was the official Year of Return of Bosnian refugees to their homes. The process of ethnic cleansing had resulted in great shifts of people leaving some no choice but to inhabit the homes of those forced to move out.

Sour Cabbage, Roses, and Lies. Slobodan: from *sloboda (slor-bor-dar) n.* freedom.

Return to Belgrade 2000. Belgrade, or Beograd*: beo* white *grad* city. The phrase *'white bone among the clouds'* is from *Return to Belgrade* by *Vasko Popa.*

Observations on Three Varieties of Snowfall. Astrakhan is lamb's wool used to make fur coats.

Reach for the Moon. A response to *Moon Is the Oldest Television* (instillation) by Nam June Paik, exhibited at the Asia Pacific Triennial, Queensland Art Gallery, 2002.

Brisbane Leaves. A response to *Brisbane Leaves* (watercolour) by Eugene Carchesio, exhibited at the Asia Pacific Triennial, Queensland Art Gallery, 2002.

Other books available in
UQP's Contemporary Poetry series

Extraction of Arrows
Kathryn Lomer

Beginning with travel days in Ireland and Spain and with glances back to childhood in rural Tasmania, this fine collection of poems maps the barbs of sexual awakening, the heart's disappointment and motherhood to arrive at relationship's harmony and self-forgiveness. Through the fragile humanity of these poems comes with a connectedness that points the direction home.

Winner of the Fellowship of Australian Writers Anne Elder Award

'Kathryn Lomer's *Extraction of Arrows* is a fine first book'.
— Martin Duwell, *Australian Book Review*

UQP Poetry
ISBN 0 7022 3371 4

The Best Australian Poetry 2004
Guest Editor, Anthony Lawrence
Series Editors, Bronwyn Lea & Martin Duwell

The Best Australian Poetry series returns after an impressive debut in 2003 with a new volume that is original, stimulating and wide-ranging in its sympathies. Guest Editor Anthony Lawrence brings to this volume a passionate commitment to Australian poetry and his reputation as one of Australia's premier poets. Bearing the impress of his distinctive editorial mind, Lawrence's selection of the best forty poems published in Australian literary journals in the preceding year is dramatic and flamboyant, revealing an unquenchable passion for life immersed in the marvellous matter of lived reality. Featuring poems by Judith Beveridge, Bruce Dawe, David Malouf, Les Murray and Margaret Scott, as well as many exciting new voices.

Praise for *The Best Australian Poetry 2003*

Guest Editor, Martin Duwell

'A portable cornucopia of fine verse … the best are here, but so are many others, and it is with them that the brightest gems have been stowed'.

— Peter Porter, *Best Books of the Year*

UQP Poetry
ISBN 0 7022 3489 3